I'm No Sleeping Beauty, You're No Prince Charming, and There's No Fairy Godmother in Sight!

Cate Howard

Dancing Dragon ◆ Nashville, Tennessee ◆1996

ISBN: 0-9650368-0-4

Cover Design: Lymbic Graphics
(615) 385-5915
Text Design: Desktop Communications
(615) 356-9542

Dancing Dragon
203 Jennings Street
Franklin, TN 37064

For interviews and other information, call
(615) 386-0133

Dedication

To Dave Gibson. Your songs touch my heart and soul—some make me smile and some make me cry, but always they inspire me.

Acknowledgments

While the existence of fairy godmothers may be in doubt, I know fairy godfathers exist—I have two. Harold McAlindon and Richard Courtney of Eggman Publishing. You guys may not carry magic wands, but you can make dreams come true.

The Eggman staff, especially Kay and Sonata. I cannot believe how good you make me look! You are the greatest!

My editor, Currey Copple. You actually made my manuscript make sense. I owe you a large box of red pencils.

A special thank you to Alice Kelly for your patience, advice and always laughing at the right time.

Bernie Nelson. You write incredible songs and have a wonderful sense of humor. Thanks for making me laugh.

My deep appreciation to Laura, David, Will and Terry Bryan. No matter how many stories I tell, Will and Terry always want to hear one more. Most of all, thanks for the use of your electricity. After Hurricane Opal swept through Birmingham, you were the only friends with power. I couldn't have completed my manuscript without your help.

Contents

I'm No Sleeping Beauty, You're No Prince Charming, and There's No Fairy Godmother in Sight!

Cate Howard

Introduction

February 1995. Bluebird Cafe, Nashville. I was listening to some great music. An unknown singer sang an unfamiliar song. I thought the song presented an interesting idea, but what if . . . . At that point my life became a scene from a movie. The song faded into the background. Everything went into soft focus. A hand (seen only by me) reached down from the ceiling and a voice (heard only by me) said, "Here is your story." Instantly I had a story, complete with beginning, middle and end. I scribbled some notes and rushed back to my motel room. I could not stop writing.

Usually when I have an idea for a story, it's only a fragment: a character, an opening line or an ending. I have to sit and plot and plan to get my characters from point A to point B. This time, I couldn't write fast enough to keep up with the ideas racing around in my head.

That night a creative barrier I didn't even realize existed was broken. On the three-hour drive home, I plotted two more stories. One of these was a variation on "The Three Little Pigs." Being a former English major, I had my little outline and character sketches. I knew exactly what I wanted to write. I began writing. But what I saw on the page was nothing like the story I had mapped out. Where in the world did that come from? I had heard authors say their characters took over and told their own stories. Oh sure, I had thought. But guess what? That's exactly what happened to me. I didn't know where that first story had come from, but I knew I was onto something. All I could do was get out of the way and let it happen.

For the next ten days I did nothing

but write. I didn't leave the house. I didn't answer the phone. I didn't feed the cat. I wrote. When I finally stopped I had the rough draft of twelve stories that became the basis of this book. Gradually my life returned to normal. Every couple of weeks I would take out the stories and work on them. Each time I read these stories, I liked them better. I love my stories!

I am a storyteller. I will tell a story anytime, anywhere, to anyone who will listen. I like funny stories. I really get on my soapbox about laughter. I don't think anyone laughs enough. Rather than taking ourselves so seriously, we need to just lighten up and get a laugh! I am always looking for stories with humor. When I began writing these stories, I was just trying to create stories I could tell that would make people laugh. Relax, sit back and have a laugh.

I want to thank all the fantastic singer-songwriters who perform at the Bluebird and Douglas Corner. They were my inspiration. It absolutely fascinates me how someone can tell a story in three minutes, make it rhyme and set it to music. Whether it makes me laugh or cry, a song has an intense emotional impact. I would listen to these artists and wonder, how do they do that? If I could create a story that carried a fourth of the emotional impact of these songs, I would have succeeded beyond my wildest dreams. The seed that grew into this book was planted at the Blue-bird in February 1995. The last story was written at Douglas Corner in September 1995.

I'm No Sleeping Beauty, You're No Prince Charming and There's No Fairy Godmother in Sight!

The title says it all. Having been raised on fairy tales, women have been led to believe a knight in shining armour would magically appear and, magically, they would live happily ever after. That put a tremendous burden on men as well as women. Women were hanging out on balconies waiting for their knights, while men were at home polishing their armour. Do you have any idea how hard it is to keep armour shiny? Let's face it. Most of us fall somewhere between the ugly stepsister/brother and Sleeping Beauty/Prince Charming. We are nice, ordinary people trying to make it through the day. I believe each of us is responsible for our own happiness. Unless we have our own acts together we will never recognize Prince/Princess Charming when he/she arrives. So stop waiting for the fairy godperson to appear carrying glass slippers (do you know how hard it is to dance in glass slippers?) and a ticket to the ball. You do not need anyone's permission to attend the ball. If you want to go, buy your own ticket and go. Just remember, Prince Charming/Sleeping Beauty will be wearing neither a crown nor glass slippers, so don't waste your time looking for something that doesn't exist. You might miss the really good stuff.

Evie Lee worked at the Minit Mart. She stacked stock, dusted displays and dreamed about Prince Charming sweeping her off her feet and taking her away from all this.

Bobby, manager of the Chicken Shack, stopped at the Minit Mart for gas every week. He asked Evie Lee to go to a movie. Evie Lee had a good time and Bobby was okay, but he smelled greasy. He was no Prince Charming. Evie Lee did not see him again.

Earl, owner of a landscaping company, stopped at the Minit Mart for soft drinks almost every day. He asked Evie Lee to go to dinner. Evie Lee had a good time and Earl was nice, but he drove a truck and cut grass. He was not Prince Charming. Evie Lee did not see him again.

Steve, a stockbroker who drove a BMW, stopped at the Minit Mart every day for a newspaper. He asked Evie Lee to a dance at the Country Club. A dance at the Country Club! That was pretty close to a fancy dress ball. Steve was as handsome as a prince, but he was not a great dancer. Rather than telling Evie Lee she was the girl of his dreams, he talked stocks, market trends and current events—things that bored Evie Lee to tears. Evie Lee was terribly disappointed, but Steve was no Prince Charming. Evie Lee did not see him again.

Evie Lee was stocking shelves, dusting displays and complaining about the shortage of Prince Charmings. Mrs.

Cate Howard

Kelly, owner of the shop next door, heard her complaining. "Evie Lee, wake up and smell the coffee!" she said. "You keep waiting for Prince Charming. Evie Lee, you are no Sleeping Beauty, and there is no Prince Charming. I am no Fairy Godmother, but I did try to help. I sent three perfectly nice young men to see you, but no one was good enough for you. You will get no more help from me. You are on your own."

Evie Lee works at the Minit Mart. She stacks stock, dusts displays and dreams about Prince Charming sweeping her off her feet and taking her away from all this.

The Three Piggettes

Why do we always think of the three pigs and wolf as males? None of them have names. Usually, none of them wear clothing. What do we really know about these characters? Nothing. We don't know their hopes, fears, dreams or favorite country singers. Do you have any idea how hard it is to find someone to do repairs on one home, much less three? This story definitely had some weak points. I decided to look at it from a different angle. Once I made the four characters female and gave them names, they took control. This is the story they told me.

Mrs. Periwinkle Pigg ... that's P-i-g-g, with two *g*'s, raised three piggettes. Having outgrown the family pen, each sister now lived in a sty of her own. The first piggette was named Priscilla Pearl Pigg. The runt of the litter, Prissy had been pampered and petted. Mrs. Pigg always rooted around and picked the best tidbits in the trough for little Prissy. Apple cores, with the seeds removed, were favorites.

Priscilla had spent this particular day under the hot, harsh glare of studio lights. Priscilla was a fashion model. I know you have seen her photograph on the covers of *Pigpolitan* and *Good Stykeeping*. Most of the other piggettes were jealous of Priscilla. They would kill to have her figure. She appeared in public on the arms of the most eligible boars. She vacationed in the south of France, where the nude beaches are.

No one understood that being beautiful was hard work. Priscilla was lying down, her hooves elevated and cucumber slices on her eyes. With a hot date that night she could not risk puffy eyes or ankles. The doorbell interrupted her beauty rest.

Peeking out the window Priscilla saw a striking young wolfette with perfect fur and makeup and wearing a lovely magenta jacket. Clutched in her paw was a business card that read, "Winifred Ward Wolf, Independent Beauty Consultant." Wini need to sell only $1,000 more to earn the bright red sports car Mitty Kitty Cosmetics awarded their top sellers. Wini had been visualizing cruising down the highway in that car, top down, tail flying in the wind. She was ready. She would not take no for an answer.

Unfortunately, this house that Wini had chosen as her first stop was surrounded by crepe myrtle. Wini was terribly allergic to crepe myrtle; it made her sneeze. Waiting for the door to open, Wini did deep-breathing exercises to calm her mounting excitement. It was a long wait because Priscilla Pigg had to make sure her mascara had not run and, of course, she could not answer the door bare-hooved. Wini was so intent on visualizing a completed sale that she did not notice the crepe myrtle until it was too late. Just as Priscilla Pigg opened the door, Wini sneezed. I do not mean a dainty, ladylike sneeze. I mean a real clear-the-sinuses sneeze. It caught Priscilla directly in the face.

This was the rudest thing to ever happen to Priscilla. She immediately slammed the door, hitting Wini in the nose. Priscilla ran to the bathroom and scrubbed her face using hot water, not warm, and soap, not gentle facial cleanser. She scrubbed until her face was a bright pink.

Wini Wolf was horrified. This situation had never been mentioned in her Mitty Kitty consultant training class. She had no idea what to do. She was sneezing so hard that all she could do was get into her car and drive away. Once the sneezing subsided Wini calmed herself and stopped the car. She did a deep-breathing exercise and a visualization before ringing another doorbell.

As luck would have it, the doorbell she rang was that of Priscilla Pigg's older sister, Patsy. Wini was concentrating so intently on breathing deeply that she did not hear the gentle tinkle of the wind chimes hung by the door.

Patsy Pigg was deep in meditation when the doorbell rang. Having only recently left a stifling, unfulfilling marriage, Patsy was going through a period of self-discovery. Her coffee table was covered with the latest self-help books: *The Porcine Prophecy, Sows Who Love Boars, Oinking to Your Inner Piglet, I'm OK, You're a Pig.* Patsy had been regressed, digressed and processed. She was serene and centered; her chakras were open. In other words, Patsy Pigg was at peace with the world.

Unfortunately, when Patsy Pigg opened her door she did not see the angel she had been expecting. What she did see was the reincarnation of the male who had, in a previous life, oppressed and suppressed her. He had berated her artistic ability, causing such grief that Patsy chose to exit that life early, never developing her full potential as an artist.

Wini immediately began her pitch: "Good afternoon. I am Winifred W. Wolf, independent Mitty Kitty beauty consultant, and I would like to sell . . . "

Patsy heard only the word "sell" and immediately lost it. Never again would she be sold a bill of goods by this . . . this . . . reincarnated male. Patsy destroyed a golden opportunity to work out differences and heal past wounds. Rather she created more bad karma, thus setting up a confrontation in a future lifetime. In other words, Patsy slammed the door. It hit Wini in the nose.

Wini could not believe this. Usually she was greeted warmly and invited in. She and her customer immediately became best friends and shared a cup of coffee while Wini presented the latest Mitty Kitty colors for eyes, lips and claws. Wini always made a sale. Thus she had quickly earned the magenta jacket and stood, poised, on the brink of owning a bright red sports car.

Wini stumbled to her dull brown sedan. Never had anyone shouted at her and called her a boar. Wini was shaken, but being the professional she was, she quickly pulled herself together, calmed her breathing and prepared to make a sale.

As she pulled into the next driveway Wini felt much better. She simply had a good feeling about this house. Inside was someone waiting to greet her with open arms and become her best friend.

I don't have to tell you this was the home of Prudence Pigg, older sister of Priscilla and Patsy. An independent Canway distributor, she needed only $500 in sales and one recruit to advance to the next level of the sales pyramid. To her, the ringing of the doorbell was opportunity knocking.

Cate Howard

The door opened, and before Wini could open her mouth, Prudence grabbed her paw and pulled her into the living room. She pushed Wini into the nearest chair and began her sales pitch.

Wini was a babe in the selling woods compared to Prudence, whom everyone said was born with a silver tongue and could sell iceboxes to Eskimos. Winifred W. Wolf never knew what hit her. An hour later, when she staggered out of Prudence Pigg's house, she had not sold one lipstick, not even an eye shadow. Rather, she had bought $500 of Canway home-cleaning products and exchanged her magenta Mitty Kitty jacket for a blue Canway blazer. Her first Canway training seminar was scheduled the following day.

You know the old saying, "Beware of the wolf in sheep's clothing." Well, I don't think you have to worry about that. There is obviously a wolf in there. What you should fear, really fear, is the piggette in a blue Canway blazer.

The Nanny Goats Three

I had so much fun with the piggettes, I decided to look for another all-male story. Then I remembered "The Billy Goats Gruff," complete with goat-eating troll. I mean, this story had everything: greed, threats, violence. I thought if I made these characters female they would find a way to get to the green grass without threats and violence. Once Geraldine appeared it was beyond my control. She is one strong-willed nanny. All I could do was get out of the way and let the story happen. It was a complete surprise to me when Jesse Goat appeared. I was not expecting him, but I sure am glad he showed up. It would have been a dull story without him.

Cate Howard

This story is set in a lovely condo perched on a hill. It is a spacious, well-appointed home, surrounded by a beautiful, well-kept lawn. The lawn should be beautiful; the yardman is paid enough to keep it that way.

It is here that lived the nanny goats three. The eldest was Geraldine, a no-nonsense, take-charge female of today. CEO of an international corporation, she made decisions involving millions of dollars and affecting thousands of lives. Having promised her mother she would look after her two younger sisters when they moved to the city, she bought the condo for them to share. Purchased when interest rates were at an all-time low, it had been a steal.

The middle sister was Beth, a sweet, quiet, serious girl. Growing up in Geraldine's shadow had not been easy.

Always deferring to Geraldine's opinion, Beth usually got lost in the crowd.
She worked in the lingerie department
of Holstein's Fine Apparel, where she
was consistently voted the most helpful employee.

Sissy, the third sister, was the baby
of the family. As the youngest she had
been spoiled rotten and always got her
way. If she didn't lots of tears were
shed. She worked part time as an aide
at a day-care center.

The grass was green and sweet for
the nanny goats three. Day followed
identical day until the day Sissy looked
out the window and spied, across the
valley, on the opposite hillside, a lovely
little cottage. Surprised she had not
noticed it before, Sissy decided she
wanted to live in that cottage. Never
mind that it was too small for the three
nannies to share. Never mind that living in the condo cost her absolutely
nothing. Never mind that she owned no
furniture and had never lived alone.

She wanted that cottage and that was that.

When her sisters arrived, she told them about her find. Beth agreed that . . . well . . . yes, it appeared to be a lovely little place. Geraldine knew all about the cottage. It had belonged to an old goat named Henry who had recently died and left the cottage to his son. The son, who lived in an apartment complex catering to young singles, was rumored to be quite a billy goat about town. Geraldine showed Sissy the listing in the real estate section of the newspaper.

After reading the ad, Sissy just knew the cottage was meant for her. She begged her sisters to go with her to look at it. Geraldine flatly refused. She was too tired to go on some wild goat chase. Beth agreed with Geraldine. After all, Geraldine always knew best. After pouting for a long time, Sissy decided she did not need her sisters to go with her. She would go alone. She dialed the number in the ad. The voice that answered sounded really cute, so Sissy made an appointment to see the cottage.

When Sissy arrived she was thrilled to be met by a handsome young buck. His fur was slicked back and his horns had been polished until they gleamed. His shirt was open to the waist, revealing a very hairy chest. He wore several gold chains, one with a tiny gold bell. Sissy was smitten.

Jesse Goat thought Sissy was pretty but very young. He could tell she was attracted by his pure animal magnetism. Because he wanted to unload the house, he turned on the charm. He had a great apartment in a complex filled with lovely nannies. In fact, he and his next-door neighbor, a stewardess for Trans-Goat Airways, planned a romp later that night. He had to get rid of this house so he could concentrate on more important things.

Jesse rolled off all the facts and

figures one does when selling a house. In spite of his appearance, Jesse had quite a head for business. Sissy, unprepared for all the facts, figures and details, was totally confused. She made an appointment for Beth to see the cottage.

Beth didn't know anything about houses. She certainly did not want to be here, but having never been able to say no to her baby sister, here she was. Jesse Goat appeared, causing Beth more distress. His cologne entered the room before he did; he called her "Babe." She knew Sissy had a crush on him, but she could not understand why. Beth made an appointment for Geraldine to see the cottage. Geraldine would have no patience with his kind; sparks would fly, and that would be the end of Jesse Goat.

Jesse had grown tired of the nanny goat sisters. All these appointments were cutting into time usually spent by the pool, and he was no closer to selling the cottage. He planned to lay on the charm with this third sister, who seemed to be the one in charge. He would sell the cottage and be done with the sisters.

Geraldine was totally stressed out. She was closing the biggest deal of her career and had neither the time nor the patience for one of Sissy's whims. Geraldine always told Mama Goat she babied Sissy too much, but Mama Goat just laughed and said, "Wait until you have kids of your own. You'll understand." That seemed unlikely now. Geraldine had buried herself in her career, and her biological clock was ticking louder each day. Geraldine felt the only kids she would ever raise were her sisters.

Having arrived early, Geraldine was checking out washer-dryer connections when Jesse appeared. Geraldine took one look and fell head-over-hooves in love. Jesse was her complete opposite: wild, free, responsible to and for no one. Her heart pounded; she found it difficult to breathe. She had never felt like this. To hide her confusion she began asking about property taxes, square footage and closet space. She appeared to be in complete control.

Jesse Goat could not believe what was happening. This nanny was not his type, but there was something about her. Usually he preferred a nanny who deferred to his opinion. Yet he was irresistibly drawn to this nanny, who was so confident and totally in charge.

Beth had been right. The sparks did fly. To cover her rising confusion and difficulty in breathing, Geraldine said, "It's a deal," and bolted from the house, hoping to regain her composure.

Two weeks later, much to everyone's surprise, Geraldine and Jesse eloped. After returning from Las Vegas they moved into the condo. Jesse opened a club that quickly became the place to meet the goat of your dreams. Geraldine began planning a large family of kids.

Because the newlyweds wanted to be alone, Beth was moved into the singles complex. Once she recovered from the shock and relaxed, she rather liked living there. No longer in Geraldine's shadow, she began to bloom. She really blossomed when she met a goat who did not wear cologne or gold chains. He did wear the tightest jeans she had ever seen. His name was Dwight.

Sissy had her lovely little cottage in a neighborhood where everyone was married with children. It appears she had learned something from her big sister. Sissy turned the cottage into a day-care center and made a killing.

They say the grass is always green on the other side of the fence. You can always find greener grass. You might find it just on the other side of the fence or you might have to move across town. Sometimes you find greener grass only after crossing the valley and climbing to the top of the next hill.

Prunella Brunhilda

Let me get this straight. The girl is ordered by the prince to turn straw into gold or she will die—not once but three times. Then she marries him! I obviously missed something because this guy does not strike me as Mr. Right. Why does the hero always have to be a prince? How many princes are wandering around out there today? Would you really want to take one of them home? What is so appealing about a prince?

I like people, real and fictional, who have original ideas and can think for themselves. I like people who use their imaginations. Carbon-copy people are real boring. So I dumped the royalty and added an original twist—or two.

Cate Howard

Margaret was an only child. Born late in her parents' lives, she had been given everything her parents thought she should have. They never failed to tell her they were giving her everything, because one day it would be her duty to take care of them.

A timid, docile child, seldom allowed out of her parents' sight, Margaret was considered a little odd by the other children. Unsure of how to make friends, Margaret spend most of her time alone, reading or lost in a world of fantasy where a handsome knight appeared and carried her off to live happily ever after, whatever *that* meant.

Margaret came by her daydreams legitimately, for her father could tell a tale better than anyone. He had been raised in a dysfunctional family and was now married to a domineering wife, so he tried to make himself feel important by exaggerating the truth.

One afternoon, in the local tavern, Margaret's father spun his greatest tale. The miller had been bragging about his son, who was learning the trade. He would one day be the greatest miller the village had ever seen; his father was sure of that. Not to be outdone, Margaret's father said that was nothing. Anyone could grind grain, but not everyone could turn acorns into gold. In fact, he knew of only one such person: his daughter, Margaret. On and on he went, spinning such a fine yarn that no one thought to ask why, if his daughter was so good at producing gold, the family wasn't rich.

Needless to say, the story spread like wildfire until it reached the village council. The village of Oak Grove had suffered a bad fiscal year. The armor factory they had hoped to attract went to a village across the river. Dragon slaying had hit a slump causing the lance factory, the village's largest employer, to lay off half its work force. Revenues were down. If the village had in its midst a person who could turn acorns into gold it would be a boon, for if there was anything the village had plenty of, it was acorns.

The council knew Margaret was different. With all the time she spent alone, maybe she was turning acorns into gold. Summoned before the august body, Margaret was told it was a time of local emergency: everyone should be using their talents to help improve the local economy. Taken to the Village Hall basement and shown a room filled with acorns, Margaret was ordered to turn the acorns into gold, just as her father said she could.

This was the first Margaret had heard of her father's tale, and she was stunned. Shut in a basement room filled with acorns, alone and totally unprepared to turn anything into gold, Margaret did the only thing she could do: cry, loudly. Her sobbing attracted the attention of the night maid, who opened the door to see what was wrong. Margaret was thrilled when the maid appeared. Thinking the door was locked and having read one too many fairy tales, Margaret believed there could be only one explanation for the appearance of this kind soul. She must be Margaret's fairy godmother.

Explaining her predicament, Margaret asked for help. She had nothing to offer in payment, she said, but when her prince came, she would be happy to richly reward her fairy godmother. The maid felt sorry for Margaret. Obviously, the child had spent too much time alone in a less than loving and supportive environment. The maid told Margaret she would be happy to help. It could not be that simple, Margaret thought. What must she do? Did the kind lady want Margaret to guess her name? This sent the maid into a fit of laughter. "You could never guess my name," she said. "I'm Prunella Brunhilda, and I'm pleased to meet you. What I want you to do is think for yourself."

Greatly relieved she did not have to come up with a name like Prunella Brunhilda, Margaret calmed down and asked how to turn acorns into gold. Prunella Brunhilda said she did not have the foggiest idea. She asked Margaret, "What talents do you have? What can you do?"

It seemed Margaret could do very little. Because her parents expected almost nothing from her, she had developed few skills. The one thing Margaret knew she could do well was cook. She appeared to have a natural talent, having made some quite tasty dishes without recipes.

"If you can cook, you can turn acorns into gold," said Prunella Brunhilda, leading Margaret down the hall to an enormous kitchen. "Think for yourself and use your imagination. What can be made from acorns?" She left Margaret alone and went to clean the council chamber.

Margaret worked all night. She had a fantastic time. No one was looking over her shoulder, telling her what to do. The kitchen was well-stocked, and she had plenty of acorns. Margaret put her well-developed imagination to good use.

The next morning the council members were drawn to the basement by the delicious smell. They entered the kitchen to find every table and counter covered with loaves of acorn bread. The bread was tasty, but they really wanted to see gold. Margaret filled their arms with bread and told them to follow her. With the council trailing behind, Margaret set out toward the armor factory across the river.

Arriving at lunch time, Margaret sold every loaf of acorn bread and took orders for more. Recognizing a good deal, the factory owner offered Margaret a contract to supply the factory on a regular basis.

To make a long story short, Margaret was a great cook and an even better businesswoman. From that one lunch-hour success, Margaret built a baking empire. She quickly became the village's largest employer and taxpayer. It appeared Margaret *could* turn acorns into gold.

Margaret bought her parents a fine mansion with a large staff to tend their every need. Margaret even found the man of her dreams. He wasn't a prince; he was a chef. They lived happily ever after. Which goes to show it doesn't matter which side your acorn bread is buttered on as long as you have someone with whom to share it.

Lucy Maud

In fairy tales every step-relative is a holy terror. I don't think that is always true and didn't want to reinforce that stereotype. I do not, however, object to the concept of a helpful fairy godmother. I have wished for mine to appear, many times. I am still waiting, by the way. However, not being able to leave well enough alone, I did make one small change that added another dimension to this story.

Lucy was a country girl who did not like living in the country. She wanted to live in the big city, drive a shiny car, wear fancy clothes and dance all night.

Lucy Maud did not like the country, but she did have old-fashioned country values. She knew that there was no such thing as a free ride, and that she would have to earn her way. Not minding hard work, she saved her money and the day after graduation took the bus to the city.

Lucy Maud was left breathless by the city. Never had she seen so much activity, so many people, so many opportunities, so much neon. Blinded by the signs, Lucy Maud soon forgot the most important lesson she had been taught: it is what you are inside, not what you own, that is important. She spent her hard-earned money on fancy clothes, a luxury apartment and a car that ran. Rather than saving, Lucy Maud spent her entire Kroger paycheck trying to get her share of all the fancy things city folk thought they needed.

Lucy Maud soon had something else she had never had before: money problems. Fortunately, she spotted an ad in the help-wanted section that read, "Maid wanted. In exchange for room and board." It was exactly what Lucy Maud needed. With free room and board and her Kroger paycheck she would have money to burn.

Lucy Maud was thrilled to learn that the ad had placed by Hortense Hunter, one of the city's leading socialites. Her name and face appeared regularly in the society columns. Often she was accompanied by her daughters, Bambi and Tawny.

Lucy Maud was dazzled by the white columns of the Hunters' antebellum mansion. Yes, this was where she was meant to be. If she could secure this position she would be on her way up-town. Unfortunately, Lucy Maud failed to realize that Hortense Hunter was looking for a maid, not another daughter. The two she had were a handful, thank you. Bambi and Tawny had been given every advantage. Sadly, not even extensive plastic surgery had notice-ably improved their looks. Let's face it, these girls were ugly enough to stop an eight-day clock. Because of their material advantages the girls found it difficult to remember they were no better than anyone else. Their attitude only made them more unattractive.

Lucy Maud was unaware that the employment agency refused to send anyone else to the Hunters because the girls had made everyone who had ever worked for them miserable. Hortense Hunter had been forced to resort to the want ads. Lucy Maud easily secured the position; she was the only applicant. Shown to the servants' quarters, she was told to always use the back door and never park her wreck of a car in front of the house.

Lucy Maud was confident that given time she would win over Bambi and Tawny. She knew they could become best friends. Clinging to this thought she never complained, questioned or hesitated to do their bidding, no matter how stupid. She ignored their rudeness and her exhaustion. Lucy Maud failed to realize that Bambi and Tawny would never want to be friends with her, if for no other reason than that Lucy Maud was twice as pretty and three times as nice as they could ever hope to be. Lucy Maud, in her desperate desire to become a part of high society, soon forgot all her childhood lessons. She lost sight of herself as a worthwhile person and saw herself only as Bambi and Tawny saw her, as a servant.

Lucy Maud worked nonstop as the Hunter household reached a fever pitch preparing for the social event of the season, a dinner-dance benefiting the Hoopnagle Facial Reconstruction Clinic, an organization near and dear to the Hunters. Lucy Maud knew anyone could attend. Anyone with plenty of money. A ticket cost $1,000 and, of course, there were the necessary extras: clothes, furs, jewels, limos, manicures and pedicures. Lucy Maud kept hoping Hortense Hunter would offer a ticket as a thank you for all the long and hard hours she had worked to help the Hunters get ready. But Lucy Maud never expressed her desire to go, and it never occurred to Hortense Hunter that Lucy Maud would want to attend.

Lucy Maud was left to clean up after Hortense Hunter, Bambi and Tawny had departed in a cloud of hair spray. Feeling really, really sorry for herself, Lucy Maud burst into tears. Suddenly the room was filled with bright light. Hopeful it was the Hunters' limo returning for her, she looked up to find a figure surrounded by white light. Lucy Maud thought it might be her fairy godmother, but when her eyes adjusted to the light she realized it was a man standing there. More than a little startled, she let out a shriek. She demanded to know who he was and how he had gotten into the house. What did he want?

Lucy was even more startled when he told her he was her fairy godfather. He explained there were as many fairy godfathers as fairy godmothers, but the godmothers tended to get better publicity. Everyone expected a god-mother, but godfathers knew how to use a magic wand, too. He was here to help Lucy Maud get what she wanted. Exactly what did she want?

Lucy Maud, having never heard of a fairy godfather, was more than a little skeptical. But if he could help her get to the social event of the season, she didn't care what he called himself. She told him she wanted to attend the dinner-dance and mingle with the who's who of society. For that she needed the right clothes; her Kroger uniform would not do. Her fairy godfather reminded her of all those clothes she had bought when she first came to the city. Rushing to the closet, Lucy Maud found that basic little black dress. One can never go wrong with basic black. Looking in the mirror she was amazed to see not Bambi and Tawny's servant, but the young girl who had come to the city full of hopes and dreams.

Lucy Maud had the clothes, but how would she get there? She could not arrive at the Rolling Hills Country Club in her old car. Her godfather reminded Lucy Maud that is why we have taxis. Hugging Lucy Maud, her godfather told her to have fun and to always remember her childhood lessons. Then he was gone, leaving behind only a ticket.

Lucy Maud created quite a stir when she arrived. Everyone wanted to meet this attractive stranger. She mixed; she mingled; she met Rod, nephew of the director of the Hoopnagle Clinic. As they gazed into each other's eyes, Rod invited Lucy Maud to accompany him to the charity badminton tournament the following weekend. Lucy Maud's feet barely touched the floor as they danced the night away.

Lucy Maud had, for a short time, lost sight of what is really important in life, but her Mama didn't raise no fool. With Rod's love and support she quickly got her feet firmly replanted on the ground. She gave notice at the Hunters'. She moved into a cheap but clean room and began saving part of her weekly Kroger paycheck. Rod was thrilled to find a girl with old-fashioned values. Lucy Maud and Rod were married and moved into a darling little house. Lucy Maud could throw a mean party, and their home soon became the place to be seen.

Lucy Maud always found time to support the Hoopnagel Facial Reconstruction Clinic, for she had learned that some people need all the help they can get. She also learned that fairy godpersons come in all shapes and sizes and disguises.

The Other Little Duckling

I strongly identify with that other little duckling. My feathers have always been considered, well, different. I searched for a long time before I found the pond where I belonged. No one likes a meek duck. Okay, I don't like a meek duck. So when the duckling gets her act together, I could not resist having her say, "I told you so!" This probably reveals a great character flaw in me, but I never said I was perfect.

Once upon a time a mother duck laid seven eggs. Numbers one through six behaved exactly as good little eggs should. They cracked open exactly on time and out popped six fuzzy cute ducklings. Exactly like every other duckling ever hatched.

Two days later, the seventh egg cracked open. Out popped what could only be described as the ugliest duckling ever hatched. No one had ever seen anything like it; no one wanted to see this one. Everyone felt terribly sorry for Mother Duck. It was obviously not her fault that something had gone horribly wrong with that one egg, but she would always bear the stigma of having hatched that "other little duckling."

Everyone felt terribly sorry for ducklings one through six. They were perfect in every way. They immediately took to the water. They loved to eat bugs and could waddle along behind Mother Duck in a perfectly straight line. The other little duckling hated the water and preferred sweet grass to crunchy bugs. The other little duckling, so clumsy she fell over her own feet, always had a scraped beak. Everyone talked about how sad it was for the six perfect ducklings to live in the same nest as that other little duckling.

No one ever felt sorry for that other little duckling. Everyone avoided her; she made them very uncomfortable. Everyone felt it would somehow make them look bad if they were seen talking to that other little duckling. She grew up alone and lonely . She would lie in the grass and look up at the clouds or the stars and dream. When she told anyone her dreams they cackled loudly. Everyone knew that the other little duckling could never do anything but sit beside the small pond.

One morning the other little duckling disappeared. No one knew where she had gone; no one really cared. Everyone was secretly relieved she was gone. Soon life on the pond returned to normal and everyone forgot that other little duckling.

One warm spring day there arrived at the pond the most attractive duck anyone had ever seen. You could have knocked over every duck there with a feather when she said, "Don't you recognize me? I'm that other little duckling."

The entire pond was quiet as she told her tale. After leaving the small pond she had settled in a larger pond where no one considered her different. She made friends who loved her odd sense of humor. She went to night school, where she discovered that she had a talent that paid very well. She learned to make the best of what she had been given and developed her own style. One day she looked in the mirror and found a very attractive duck—one who was unique, not ugly.

The other little duckling wanted to thank everyone for making her leave the pond. If she had felt wanted, she would have built a nest beside the small pond and grown old there. Because everyone had made it very clear she was not like everyone else, and therefore not wanted, she had left. She had found a pond where she was welcomed, appreciated and loved. She had returned to say to those who had laughed at her dreams, "I told you so!"

We have all heard that birds of a feather flock together. That's fine if your feathers match everyone else's feathers. If, however, you have odd feathers, leave the flock and find a pond where no one cares how your feathers look. It is better to be a happy bird in a large pond than an unhappy bird in a small pond.

A Fish Tale
(or How to Make a Star Fish)

Fairy tale couples are either disgustingly happy or act as if they really can't stand each other. The wife is a shrew and the husband henpecked. One is completely right and the other totally wrong. One is smart; the other as dumb as a dog biscuit. I thought it would be nice to tell a story in which the husband and wife care about one another and are accepting of the other's strengths and shortcomings. Neither person in this story is wrong. It just happens the wife is incredibly resourceful.

At the edge of the sea lived a fisherman and his wife. Each morning the fisherman would go down to the sea and cast his line. He would take his catch into the village and sell it. Thus the couple was able to live.

It was an uncertain life. There weren't fish to sell everyday. Even on the days there were fish the fisherman might decide he would rather sit by the sea and watch the waves than walk into the village. Other days he would start toward the village only to be distracted by the least thing—cloud shapes in the sky or oddly colored rocks in the road— and never reach the village. The fisherman was a dreamer.

The fisherman's wife found it difficult to live with a dreamer. She loved her husband; he was a good man but not a good provider. The wife had no illusions about living in a castle or wearing jewels. She wanted only to have enough to live comfortably and not constantly worry about paying the bills. She would like to be able to buy something to eat besides fish. Some air freshener would also be nice.

One day the wife went to the cupboard only to find it bare, with not even a bone for the dog. Sorry, that's another story. The cupboard *was* empty. She stressed to her husband how serious this was; he really must sell a fish today. When he had not returned after several hours, she realized she would have to do something.

She took the net and went down to the sea. In no time she caught an enormous fish, the biggest she had ever seen. She knew she could get a good price for it in the village. As she reached to remove it from the net, the fish spoke. He opened his mouth and out came crystal-clear words. He told the fisherman's wife he would grant her a wish, if only she would return him to the sea.

After the woman stopped shaking and began breathing again, she realized she had something here. It is not every day you find a talking fish. People would pay to talk to a fish. They would pay well. The fish tried to reason with her. He tried to bribe her. He offered two wishes, three wishes. She could have anything she wanted, free, just for a wish—no work involved.

The fisherman's wife explained she didn't have much faith in wishes. She was much more comfortable with working and earning something than with just sitting and wishing. But she was not an unkind woman and did not want to take advantage of the fish or cause distress. She did realize that, as a fish, he probably was more comfortable in the water.

After getting the fish a bucket of water, the fisherman's wife asked if they could work out a compromise. They could travel to nearby villages, maybe work up a little comedy routine, and charge a few pennies. In only a short time they could make enough money for her and her husband to live comfortably for the rest of their lives. It would not have to be a permanent arrangement. There must be something the fish wanted or needed. Even fish have needs.

The fish thought for a moment and replied that there was one thing. The sea could get awfully cold during the winter. If they could do this in the winter and have a tank with tepid water, not hot, but warmer than sea water, he would certainly be interested.

Each winter thereafter "The Talking Fish Comedy Revue" could be seen throughout out the land. The fish knew some great fish tales. He also had a delightful sense of humor ... for a fish. His reputation spread, and what had been a plain, albeit talking, fish soon became a star fish. The fish had a warm winter home. The fisherman's wife had enough money for her husband and her to live comfortably. The fisherman was free to sit and watch the clouds by day and the stars by night. They were all very happy.

This only goes to show that, while you may not want to look a gift horse in the mouth, you might want to listen when a fish speaks.

The Princess and the Minstrel

Talk about stereotypes! A princess so delicate she can feel a pea under twenty-odd mattresses and so stupid she would actually climb on top of twenty-odd mattresses to sleep. I eliminated the pea and the mattresses and put the princess in charge. She is under pressure to conform to the norm, but she has a mind of her own and uses it. She knows what she wants and will not settle for less. I knew the princess was not riding off into the sunset with a prince, but I could not decide whom she would choose. Who would be the most unlikely candidate for a princess? A singer. Most women have dreamed of being swept off their feet by their favorite singer. Why wouldn't this work for a princess? That would certainly throw a monkey wrench into the best-laid royal plans. It works for me.

Princess Elaine was a true princess, beautiful and kind. As her father's eldest child she would one day inherit his kingdom. Therefore, she had many suitors. Every knight, prince and baron sought her hand, but each was lacking the quality Princess Elaine wanted in a husband.

The king loved his daughter and could refuse her nothing, but he was beginning to believe Princess Elaine would never find a husband. She had earned a reputation as a very difficult woman. He, like everyone else, knew a princess, no matter how beautiful or kind, needed a husband. He kept asking exactly what she wanted.

No one would have understood had Princess Elaine explained what she wanted. She was looking for a man with whom she could talk, discuss issues, exchange ideas. She wanted a man who would not be intimidated by her intelligence. No one really wanted an intelligent princess, not even if she would one day rule the kingdom. After all, there were advisors and ministers to handle the royal business. It was not necessary for the princess to have opinions or ideas.

Each suitor could only boast of his accomplishments: his valor in battle, great wealth, the number of pounds he could bench-press. Not one of the suitors could put together two sentences and carry on a meaningful conversation, so they certainly did not expect, or want, that quality in a potential wife. Princess Elaine simply wanted a man who had as much interest in her IQ as in her acreage.

Every year a great tournament was held. For three days, knights and king-wannabes from far and wide waged contests of skill, strength and physical agility. Each came not only to win honor and glory but also hoping he would be the one to capture the princess' heart. Princess Elaine would smile as each knight presented himself, bowed before her and flexed his muscles while displaying his weapons. No one would have guessed she was bored to tears; she had no interest in sports. She attended only because it was her royal duty.

Each night of the tournament a banquet was held in the castle's great hall. The day's highest scoring knights were seated on either side of the princess. Each did his best to impress Princess Elaine. He would regale her with his battle statistics: number of dragons slain, giants killed, damsels rescued, villages defended, interceptions and touchdowns. Neither thought of allowing Princess Elaine to actually say anything. She was expected only to ooh and aah. Had the princess been allowed to speak, the knights would have been stunned by the question she would have asked: Read any good books lately?

The entertainment for the banquet was a minstrel who played the lute, sang songs and told stories. Few people paid any attention; no one actually listened to what he said. No one, that is , except Princess Elaine. Here was a man who could put together more than two sentences, in rhyme, with music. Here was a man she wanted to meet. Here was a man she wanted to talk to.

Princess Elaine summoned the minstrel to her chambers. Hopeful, but not really expecting anything, the princess waited. True, the minstrel could write songs, but could he carry on a conversation—with a princess?

The minstrel was not surprised by the princess' interest. He was as accustomed to royal summonses as squeals from the village girls when he performed at local fairs. Every woman fell in love with him and wanted him to write a song just for her. Princesses were no exception. He fully expected this princess to simper, giggle and find it hard to breathe in his presence. The last thing he expected was someone with whom he could talk, someone who was interested in his ideas and opinions.

Both Princess Elaine and the minstrel, whose name was Dave, were amazed to learn that the other could put together several sentences on a wide range of topics. They read the same books, enjoyed the same music and were concerned about the destruction of the eagles' nesting grounds. Dave played a song he was composing and discovered Elaine had an ear for music. They completed the song together.

The next day everyone commented on how unusually happy Princess Elaine looked. That night no one gave it a thought when the minstrel dedicated his new song to the princess.

The tournament over, everyone began packing for the journey home. It appeared that, once again, no knight had won the princess' heart, much to the king's sorrow. Imagine the king's surprise and shock when his daughter and the minstrel appeared before him to announce they had fallen in love and wanted his permission to marry. Good Lord, the princess wanted to marry a minstrel!

Princess Elaine told her father she wished to renounce her claim to the throne in favor of her younger brother. The prince was a very capable young man who would one day be a great king. Having a king, rather than a queen, on the throne would make everyone very happy. Besides, she loved Dave.

Dave explained that he could provide very well for Elaine. In addition to a good income from his music he had a large country estate. Elaine would want for nothing. More important, he loved Elaine.

While this was hardly the man the

king would have chosen for his daughter, it was obvious Elaine was happy. The king was greatly relieved she had finally found a husband. He granted permission for them to wed.

Elaine and Dave were married. They read books, had deep intense conversations, laughed and made beautiful music together the rest of their lives. This just proves that knights in shining armor don't always come in full battle dress. Sometimes they are armed with a lute rather than a lance.

The Goosey Princesses
(or Honk If You Love Me)

You can't always make every character noble and lovable. There is no getting around the fact that some people are naturally obnoxious. The two princesses fall into that category. All I could do was make it funny and show that some people have to learn their lessons the hard way. Hey, no one said life was easy.

The two princesses in question were attractive, as far as appearances go. They were not attractive inside. You know the old saying, "Pretty is as pretty does." Well, these two were not considered pretty because each had a mean streak a mile wide. Everyone had become accustomed to the princesses' shouting and rudeness: *please* and *thank you* were not in their vocabulary. But it was not only their rudeness that made them unattractive. They went out of their way to make everyone miserable. They dropped a bar of soap in front of the chamber maid as she carried pails of water, so the maid and water went everywhere. They tripped the serving girl as she carried trays of food, so the serving girl and food went everywhere. The princesses never said they were sorry. In fact, they laughed until tears rolled down their cheeks.

Not even the castle animals were spared the princesses' meanness. Burrs were put under the saddles of the riding horses. The cat's milk bowl was overturned and the dog's favorite bone tossed into the trash.

Everyone, human and animal, was sick of the princesses' behavior. The king was bewildered by the way his daughters acted. He tried pleading, threatening and locking them in their rooms; nothing had any effect. He decided the only course of action was to marry off the princesses. At least then they would be someone else's problem and everyone in his kingdom would have some peace. He had portraits painted and sent to the most distant kingdoms with eligible princes. He hoped stories of the princesses' behavior had not spread beyond the boundaries of his kingdom. The king was in luck. He received an offer of marriage from sibling princes. Oh, joy, joy, joy! There was hope after all, if the princesses would just behave until after the weddings.

Everyone in the kingdom was ecstatic and began preparing for the arrival of the princes. Everyone except the princesses. It was nastiness as usual for them. Their targets this day were the geese in the palace pond. The princesses loved throwing rocks at the geese and watching them scatter. Usually the geese would fly away, but now, with a flock of goslings, that was impossible for Mother Goose. The pitiless princesses pelted the petite poultry with pebbles and laughed like loons when Mother Goose honked at them, "You will truly regret this!" How could a mere goose make them regret anything?

The next morning, the very day the two princes were to arrive, the princesses awoke feeling very strange. How they felt was nothing compared with how they looked. They were covered in feathers from head to toe ... er ... beak to webbed feet. Yes, each had orange beak and feet. They were complete geese.

When the chambermaid arrived with breakfast, she was amazed to find two geese rather than two princesses. She could not understand how the geese had gotten into the bed chamber. The geese were taken outside and put into the pond. You would have thought they were drowning by the noise they made. The princesses were screaming because they had never been in cold water before. To everyone else, it sounded like geese honking.

No one could figure out what happened to the two princesses. It would, of course, be hard to explain to the princes when they arrived and found no brides, but no one was terribly concerned about that right now. They were too busy enjoying the peace and quiet.

The two wild geese, however, were making everyone miserable, just the princesses had. They were chasing after everyone, honking that they were really princesses, not geese. Not even throwing water and rocks at the geese would shut them up. Their honking quickly grated on everyone's nerves.

The two prince bridegrooms arrived in the afternoon. The two geese . . . er . . . princesses spied them entering the castle. Ohhh, let me tell you, the princes were *fine*! The two princesses' little goose hearts went pitter-pat. They ran toward the princes, honking wildly, trying to identify themselves as the princes' future brides. This was too much for the king. He ordered the cook to catch the two wild geese and serve them for dinner. The princes would have a good meal before they learned their brides had disappeared.

The cook sent the kitchen maid to catch the geese and … well … you know … do what you must do before putting geese in an oven and roasting them. When the maid caught the geese she decided it would be a shame to waste such lovely downy feathers. Those feathers would make a soft down pillow, she thought, so she started plucking them. The geese squawked louder than ever, but feathers kept flying. When the maid finished she was startled to see, standing before her, two plucked princesses. Yup, they were naked as jaybirds and bald as billiard balls, not a hair on their heads. The maid began to laugh. She laughed until tears ran down her cheeks. The princesses just ran.

That night at dinner, a great silence fell across the hall when the princesses made a fashionably late entrance. Everyone was stunned. Everyone from the castle had thought they had seen the last of the princesses. The princes found the princesses even more beautiful than their portraits, even with those most unusual turbans on their heads. The princesses were gracious, kind and mannerly. They requested vegetable plates.

The princes and princesses were married and rode off to their new home, taking with them the kitchen maid and her soft feather pillow.

Remember, it is fine to feather your nest, but be careful your goose isn't cooked in the process.

Jacqueline and the Beanstalk

A cow for a handful of dried beans? I don't think so. No woman would accept that trade; she would know it was no bargain. Why has no one ever noticed there are beans on the beanstalk? Talk about not seeing the forest for the trees. Whey does there always have to be a giant, a man-eating giant at that? Sometimes to reach the stars you have to keep your feet firmly planted on the ground.

Jacqueline and her mother lived in a small cottage west of the village. The two women lived a hard, but not unpleasant, life. They grew vegetables that they sold in the market. This had not been a good year. Because of a lack of rain, there were few vegetables to sell and money was scarce. They had no choice but to sell their cow.

As Jacqueline led the cow toward the market, she met a little old woman. Upon hearing the cow was for sale, the woman offered Jacqueline an unbelievable deal: a handful of beans in exchange for the cow. Of course, these were not ordinary beans; they were magic beans. Jacqueline, being of sound mind and good intelligence, laughed hysterically and asked if many people accepted her offer. The woman said she had little success. Her husband was the one who could always find a sucker . . . er, make a deal. When Jacqueline and the little old woman parted, the woman had the cow. Jacqueline had a handful of beans, and a pocketful of silver.

Upon her return home, Jacqueline planted the beans. It couldn't hurt. If they were magic they might grow where nothing else would.

Imagine Jacqueline's surprise when she awoke the next morning to find an enormous beanstalk outside her window. The base of the beanstalk was larger than the cottage. The beans hanging from the beanstalk were taller than Jacqueline. One bean could feed a family of five for a month. Of course, who would want to eat nothing but beans for a month?

Jacqueline's fortune was made. Because it sprang from a magic bean, the beanstalk produced year-round. Jacqueline opened a processing plant and "Jacqueline's Magic Green Beans" were shipped throughout the land. Jacqueline became the Bean Queen, and also rich.

The giant beanstalk became a tourist attraction. People were eager to pay for the privilege to be the first to climb to the top of the beanstalk, which disappeared into the clouds. Of course, no one ever succeeded in reaching the top. Jacqueline never tried. She had made her fortune by keeping her feet planted firmly on solid ground and had no need to climb a beanstalk.

Besides, Jacqueline was afraid of heights.

The Bird with the Golden Feathers

It amazes me how many fairy tales end with a woman and a man who have just met, complete strangers, riding off into the sunset. The implication is they will live happily ever after and everything will be peachy keen. Seldom is everything peachy keen. Any relationship requires hard work. I wanted, just once, for a woman to say no thanks and not accept the first thing that came along. This story is also about laughter. Just lighten up! There are few situations that cannot be improved by a little laughter. Let's face it, if you are stuck to a squawking bird you'd better be able to laugh.

Cate Howard

A poor widow lived with her three daughters at the edge of a forest. Each day the daughters went into the forest to fetch wood for the fire.

Early one morning the eldest girl, Amelia, went into the forest. A very lazy girl, she would gather only branches lying on the ground. Suddenly, a little old woman appeared and offered her help. Amelia rudely told the woman she needed help from no one and to be on her way.

At midday the second daughter, Bedelia, went for wood. Being a bit less lazy than her sister she would break off small limbs as long as no great effort was required. The little old woman appeared and offered her help. Bedelia informed her she was quite capable of doing it herself.

When it was time to prepare supper

the youngest daughter, Clarice, was sent for wood. Being an industrious and reliable girl, she took the ax and went into the forest. When she finished cutting the wood, night had fallen. The little old woman appeared and offered her help. Clarice said she was not sure of the way home in the dark. If the little old woman could help her find her way, she would be Clarice's guest for super.

After pointing the way, the little old woman told Clarice that because she, unlike her sisters, had shown kindness, she would be rewarded. Clarice should look in the hollow tree, take what she found and seek her way in the world. She should not return home because ill fortune awaited her there.

In the hollow tree Clarice found a bird covered with golden feathers. Turning to say thank you, she found the little old woman had vanished. Even though warned not to return home, Clarice felt she must. Despite their harsh treatment, Clarice was sure her mother and sisters would worry if she did not return. So Clarice, being a dutiful girl, took the wood and the bird and headed home.

When Clarice entered the house with the golden bird, her sisters became so jealous they tried to take it from her. Amelia and Bedelia grabbed the bird; both stuck tight. Their mother tried to free them; she stuck tight. Clarice had found this wonderful bird, but now Amelia, Bedelia and their mother were firmly attached to it. Nothing Clarice tried could free them, so there they remained all night. Between her sisters' moans and mother's groans and the bird's squawks, Clarice got no sleep. Clarice now wished she had heeded the little old woman's advice.

The next morning Clarice took her golden bird with attached two sisters and mother and set out to find the little old woman. It was difficult to tell who was squawking loudest, the two sisters, the mother or the bird. Upon entering the forest they met a woodsman. Seeing the great distress of the two sisters, the mother and the bird, and not heeding Clarice's warning, the woodsman attempted to separate them. Clarice continued on her way, holding the bird with attached two sisters, mother and woodsman.

Deeper in the forest they met a hunter. Hearing the pitiful cries and ignoring Clarice's warning, the hunter tried to free them. Clarice continued down the path, holding the bird with attached two sisters, mother, woodsman and hunter.

Out of the forest and approaching a village, they came upon a father and son headed for market. Hearing the terrible cries and pleas for help, and ignoring Clarice's advice, the father and son attempted to free those stuck to the bird. Clarice entered the village holding the bird with attached two sisters, mother, woodsman, hunter, father and son. In the village they met the mayor and his wife and her pet dog. Learning they did not have a parade permit, the mayor and his wife attempted to disperse the crowd. Clarice reached the town square holding the bird with attached two sisters, mother, woodsman, hunter, father, son, mayor, wife and dog. The bird was squawking, the people moaning and groaning, and the dog barking.

The mayor and his wife had a son, a strapping lad. He had been given every advantage money could buy, yet he was not happy. He could see only the dark side of every situation. Finding no pleasure in life, he never smiled or laughed. This lad was standing in the village square when Clarice appeared, holding the bird with attached two sisters, mother, woodsman, hunter, father, son, mayor, wife and dog. This struck the lad as unbelievably funny. He began laughing and could not stop.

As soon as the lad began laughing the parade stopped. Looking at themselves and realizing how silly they looked, everyone stuck to the bird began laughing. As soon as they stopped complaining and started laughing, the spell was broken and they were freed from the bird.

When the lad stopped laughing, he asked Clarice to be his bride. He told her he could provide well for her and was sure they would be very happy. This struck Clarice as unbelievably funny. She began laughing and could not stop. At last she was able to tell the lad she was not about to marry a total stranger. She had the bird with the golden feathers and could provide for herself.

Clarice and the bird with the golden feathers settled in a cottage at the edge of the forest. There they lived comfortably, happily and humorously. Clarice had learned that material wealth is nice, but no one is truly wealthy until he can laugh long and honestly.

Blue Piper

I don't like the idea of children paying for the mistakes of adults. I decided to let the man in charge, the one responsible for the mess, be the one who was punished. When all is said and done, sometimes it just takes a woman to get the job done.

Rats! Rats! Rats! Everywhere you looked there were rats. Teeny, tiny rats, medium rats, big rats, huge unbelievably large and disgustingly gross rats. Everywhere! You could not walk without stepping on rats. Sitting down, you sat on rats. Pulling back the bed covers, you found rats. When you opened the kitchen cupboard, out jumped rats. Rats! Rats! Rats! Everywhere you looked there were rats.

This was the situation in the village, and the situation was bad! Of course, they had tried traps. Rat traps were everywhere, but the rats had long ago learned to avoid them. Now the rats would walk by a trap and laugh, Ha! Of course, they could not use poison; there were children and pets in the village. Yes, there were cats and dogs, but the rats had long ago lost their fear of the larger animals. In fact, some of the rats were almost as large as the cats. The rats would walk by a cat or dog and laugh, Ha!

Yes, experts had been consulted. Nationally known rat trappers, pest control experts with guaranteed formulas, rat catchers with traps and locks and boxes— all had attempted to de-rodent the village. All had failed, miserably.

How, you may ask, did such a problem come to be? It is quite simple: substandard construction. In those days there were no sealed bids, contracts, specifications. The village mayor decided his brother-in-law was just the man to build the village sewage system.

Why, you may ask, did the mayor select his brother-in-law? What qualifications did he have? None, except being married to the mayor's baby sister. Plus he worked cheap. If there was one thing the mayor loved more than his baby sister, it was a deal. The mayor could hold onto a coin so tightly he left fingerprints embedded in the coin. The mayor was cheap and always on the lookout for a deal.

While the mayor was looking for a deal, the rat population was growing. Also growing was the citizens' dissatisfaction. They were in danger of being overtaken by rats if something was not done soon. A recent editorial in the village newspaper had suggested it was time for a change in village leadership. Rebellion was in the air.

That was the situation the day a large blue wagon rolled into the village square. Written on the side of the wagon was "Blue Piper, Professional Pest Persuader and Prestidigitator." Driving the wagon was an attractive young woman dressed in blue. Stopping the wagon, the young woman pulled out a flute and piped a merry tune. She introduced herself as Blue Piper. She had come to rid the village of all its rats.

Blue Piper was taken to the mayor, who demanded to know how she, a mere woman, could do what no one else, no man, had been able to do. Blue Piper simply smiled and said it was all in her pipe. With it she would persuade the rats to leave; she would make them an offer they could not refuse. For a single dollar per rodent she would remove all the rats from the village. If one rat remained there would be no charge.

Talk about a deal! This one was near and dear to the mayor's heart. (This is giving him the benefit of the doubt and saying he had a heart.) Possibly this woman could remove some of the rats, but there was no way she could remove all of them. Therefore, it would cost nothing. It was an offer the mayor could not refuse.

Blue Piper told everyone to remain inside that night and in the morning all the rats would be gone. Everyone went to bed with the sound of Blue Piper's flute filling the streets. Villagers fell asleep with rats nibbling on their toes and awoke to find . . . no rats! Everyone was amazed to find no rats on the kitchen table, no rats in the bathtub, no rats on the front porch, no rats in the streets, no rats anywhere in the village.

Everyone rushed to the village square. They could not wait to see the mayor's face as he handed all that money to Blue Piper. They found Blue Piper and her blue wagon. She was waiting to be paid the money she had earned.

The mayor did not appear. Blue Piper and the villagers waited. When the mayor failed to arrive, the villagers went looking for him. The village was searched from top to bottom; no stone was left unturned. Just like the rats, the mayor had disappeared.

The villagers were shocked, then thrilled. With the rats gone this was a different village. It needed a different leader. Blue Piper had solved both of the village's problems. The villagers happily paid Blue Piper the money she had earned. Blue Piper and her blue wagon drove away, leaving only the sound of her pipe.

No one ever learned what happened to the mayor. Some said the sound of Blue Piper's flute drove away the big rat. Others said he was driven away by the idea of paying Blue Piper all that money. Everyone agreed Blue Piper had done exactly what she promised. She had rid the village of all its rats.

Everyone knows that money cannot buy happiness. It can, however, pay for peace from pests, human and animal, large and small.

Roxy

I thought I went to the Bluebird to listen to the music, but I was wrong. I went so I would meet Jeanne and Taylor. We started talking and of course I told them about my book. Jeanne said, "Please write a story dispelling the dumb-blonde myth." Having been a natural brunette and, after discovering Miss Clairol, a redhead, I had never given much thought to blondes, but as we talked I got this idea.

It was not Roxy's fault she was shut away in an ivory tower. The events that put her there had been set in motion long before her birth. Roxy's mother was a beautiful woman, with ice-blue eyes and long blonde hair. Because of her physical appearance her family and friends considered her delicate and needy of protection and guidance. Even after she became an adult everyone spoke to her in tones they would use with a child. No one ever asked her opinion because no one thought she could possibly have one. After years of such treatment she no longer had an opinion. She had become exactly what everyone considered her to be, a not-quite-bright blonde.

Next to Roxy's parents lived a powerful magician. Her garden was filled with fruit trees. Roxy's mother dearly loved pears, so she helped herself. She never thought to ask permission. She had never been denied anything; why would she be denied this? When the magician saw what had happened, she asked, in exchange for the fruit, to be the godmother of the first child born to Roxy's mother. That struck Roxy's mother as a fair bargain, so she agreed.

It was only after she told her husband of the agreement and he became upset that she began to doubt the wisdom of her promise. The more she thought about it, the more she doubted her decision-making ability and became convinced she had made a terrible mistake. She did not calmly discuss her fears with the magician. She simply pretended the promise had never been made. When Roxy was born, no announcement was sent to the magician. No invitation to the baby's christening was delivered. Roxy's mother ignored the situation and expected it to go away.

The magician, unaccustomed to broken promises, was highly miffed, and a miffed magician is a dangerous magician. She neither discussed her hurt feelings with Roxy's mother nor ignored the situation, hoping it would go away. She took revenge. She took baby Roxy. Roxy was settled in an ivory tower in the middle of the forest. Here she grew up in luxury. She had every-

Cate Howard

thing she needed except family and
friends. The magician gave Roxy a good
education and many books to read.
Roxy looked at the pictures and wondered what it would be like to have a
family and a home where she was loved
and allowed to come and go freely.

Roxy was a pretty baby who grew
into a lovely girl and a beautiful young
woman. She had ice-blue eyes and long
blonde hair; she looked just like her
mother. For this reason the magician,
even with her gift of second sight, never
saw beyond Roxy's exterior. She saw
blonde hair and thought the child was
probably just like her mother, not very
bright. When Roxy asked questions
about home and family and freedom,
the magician laughed and answered
flippantly, usually in words of one or
two syllables she thought Roxy could
easily understand.

The more unanswered questions
Roxy asked the more dissatisfied she
became. She was positive there was

something wonderful and exciting waiting outside her ivory tower. She wasn't sure she wanted to spend her life in that unknown world; she just wanted to know what was out there. The magician refused to let Roxy leave the tower, even in her company.

One day the magician arrived at the tower to find the door standing open. She rushed in to discover the tower empty. Lying on the floor was a book entitled *95 Ways to Pick a Lock.*

Losing the one person she was sure she would never lose, the magician learned the hard way you don't lock someone you love in an ivory tower. Neither do you judge someone by stereotypes perpetuated by the media. She realized much too late that rather than being a dumb blonde, Roxy was one smart cookie.

Ruby Begonia

I have always been turned off by the traditional fairy tale heroes. They usually look like they are twelve years old with no life experience, not one line on their faces. Usually, they have that blond Dutch boy haircut, with bangs. Don't even get me started on their clothes! The character I was drawn to was the woodsman in "Snow White." He had long dark hair and a beard. (I think every man should have a beard.) He wore the medieval equivalent of blue jeans. Plus, he turned out to be a nice guy, a real hero. That was my idea of someone with whom to ride off into the sunset. As soon as I said that, I knew I had a story.

Ruby Begonia's life was pretty perfect. She was charming, sweet, beautiful and a princess. As the king's daughter she had the run of the castle and kingdom. She knew everyone, and everyone knew and loved her. Even though she was a princess, Ruby Begonia never put on airs or acted as if she were better than anyone else. Ruby Begonia was as happy in the forest as the castle. She loved wandering among the trees and would sit for hours making friends with the forest animals. Ruby Begonia's life was pretty perfect.

Until her father remarried. That did not bother Ruby Begonia; she was happy to see her father so happy. The new queen was not much older than Ruby Begonia. Now, Ruby Begonia had no problem with that, but the new queen did. She was a very beautiful woman, accustomed to leaving everyone breathless by her beauty. She did not like sharing the spotlight with anyone, particularly a princess who did not act like a princess and preferred the company of forest animals to that of other royalty. As Ruby Begonia grew older and more beautiful, things grew worse. The situation really became tense when young men began courting Ruby Begonia. Being polite princes, they called the queen "ma'am." She did not like being called "ma'am." She was not old enough to be a "ma'am." There could be only one solution. Ruby Begonia had to go

A royal decree was published. It stated that Princess Ruby Begonia would be leaving shortly to attend a distant prestigious finishing school, the same prestigious finishing school that had produced the queen. The news saddened everyone in the kingdom; they hated to see Ruby Begonia go. No one was more unhappy than Ruby Begonia. Not only did she not want to leave the kingdom, but she did not feel she needed finishing. Particularly if that meant she would be as proud and vain as the queen.

The weeks after the announcement were filled with preparations, polishing and pruning. The queen was determined that Ruby Begonia be presentable (i.e., look like a princess) and not reflect badly upon the queen. After all, she was one of the school's most famous alumna and had an image to uphold. One day, in order to escape the frenzy, Ruby Begonia went walking in the forest. Being with the animals always made her happy, and soon she would no longer be able to spend time with them. In the forest Ruby Begonia ran into Rufus, the groundskeeper. She had known him all of her life. His father had been groundskeeper before him, and Rufus and Ruby Begonia had grown up playing together in the forest. Never before had he seen Ruby Begonia so unhappy, and it distressed him greatly.

They spent a happy afternoon together, and Rufus urged Ruby Begonia to return anytime she needed to talk to someone.

In the following weeks Ruby Begonia returned often. She found she was much more at ease with Rufus than with the royal suitors over whom she was expected to swoon. Not only was he much nicer than the princes, but he was also much more attractive and not afraid of manual labor. The hardest thing a prince ever did was compose a sonnet, and most of those were really bad. Ruby Begonia fell in love.

Rufus asked Ruby Begonia to marry him. True, he was not a prince, but he did love Ruby Begonia and would do his best to care for her. She would not have to leave the kingdom, but she would no longer be in the same castle as the queen. Not terribly interested in being a princess anyway, Ruby Begonia said yes.

The king, knowing Rufus was a good

man who would be a good husband, was glad to see Ruby Begonia so happy. The queen, not believing any princess would willingly move from a castle to a groundskeeper's cottage and having no idea how to explain that to the prestigious finishing school, fell into a stupor. She had to remain in bed for many days. She was so prostrate she was unable to attend the wedding. No one missed her.

This just proves that what you are looking for might be right under your nose and when your prince arrives he probably won't be riding a white horse— or wearing a crown.

The Bears and Ms. Locke

This story grew from the words "Baby Bernie Bear." They popped into my head and I had to use them. I had not planned to do a bear story, but I had this great name, Baby Bernie Bear; it just rolls off your tongue. If that is the baby, what would Daddy and Mama be named? Buford and Betty, of course. I searched all of my "name the baby" books, but no other names worked. I had Buford and Betty and Baby Bernie Bear and they had a story to tell. Here it is.

The Bear family was messy. Daddy Buford Bear was an inventor. He was always in the process of taking something apart and putting something else together. He had bits and pieces of odds and ends scattered everywhere. Mama Betty Bear wrote an advice column for the newspaper. She had papers and letters and books on everything from afghans to zwieback stacked everywhere. Baby Bernie Bear was a baby, a cute baby. He had blocks and trucks and diapers all over the house. He left a trail of crumbs everywhere.

Quite happy with their messy house, the Bears never thought of it as messy. They considered it a well-lived-in home. It never bothered them if a hammer or dictionary or rubber duck was in the middle of the floor. They just stepped over it. They were not disturbed if their favorite chair was broken. With a little duct tape Daddy Buford Bear could fix anything. They did not worry about unmade beds. After all, they would crawl right back into them that night. They did not lose their cool if their soup came out of the pot too hot. They went for a walk while it cooled.

One noon the soup was very hot and the Bears took a walk while it cooled. During their absence, Ms. Locke, a representative of the Maid for You Agency, knocked on their door. Not having been closed securely, the door came open. Ms. Locke was shocked by the mess that greeted her. Here was a house aching for attention, begging for a broom and crying for a cleaning. She became a woman with a mission and forgot she had not been invited into the Bears' home. Rushing to her car she returned with brooms, brushes, polish and toolbox.

Upon their return the Bears thought they had walked into someone else's house. The blinds were dust-free, dishes washed and crumbs swept away. Daddy Buford Bear's chair was no longer held together with duct tape. The broken leg had been properly repaired with glue and a nail. Mama Betty Bear's desk was covered with neat, orderly stacks of paper. Right there on top was the roach-kill recipe she had been looking for. Baby Bernie Bear found his favorite toy, a drum. It had been missing for a very long time and there it was, in the toy box.

Hearing a noise the Bears rushed upstairs to find Ms. Locke putting clean sheets on their beds. Wrapped up in her work, Ms. Locke did not hear the Bears come up the stairs and was quite startled when they entered the bedroom. She let out a small scream. Then she realized she was the one out of place, having entered the Bears' home without permission. She apologized profusely for her intrusion and said, of course, there would be no charge for her service.

The Bears were amazed. They had never thought about hiring a maid. It was much easier to find things in a clean house. They would have more time for the things they loved: tinkering, writing and playing. They apologized for frightening Ms. Locke and inquired about the cost of her service.

Thereafter Ms. Locke came to the Bears' house once a week. Ms. Locke loved a messy house; she saw it as a challenge. The Bears loved a clean house, as long as they weren't the ones cleaning. Everyone was very happy with their arrangement.

When a door opens, at least look at what is on the other side. You might find exactly what you have been seeking. After all, one person's trash is another's treasure.

Little Red and Dirty Dan McWolfe

Now for something completely different. We have had stories set in condos, castles and cottages. We have been inside too long. We need to go outside and get some fresh air and sunshine. We need some wide open paces where men are men and women like them anyway. Let's mosey on out west.

This here is the tale 'bout the school marm, Deputy Dixon and Dirty Dan McWolfe. Ever word is true as the day is long. You can believe it or not. 'Tain't no hair off my hide if you don't.

It all commenced early one morning with Little Red, Dry Gulch's school marm, moseying along to set a spell with her Granny out at the Lazy A Spread. Now the Lazy A was way out of town. It was plum on t'other side of the train depot.

Little Red was called Little Red 'cause her Mama was called Big Red. Her Mama was called Big Red 'cause she had a head full of the brightest red hair anybody had ever seen. So when Big Red had a baby girl with that same red hair she naturally got tagged Little Red. That was fine with Little Red 'cause she woulda whupped anybody, man or woman, boy or girl, who tried to call her by her given name, Eugenia Edith. Can't say as I blame her.

Anyway, Little Red was moseying on out to the Lazy A to set a spell with her Granny, who had been a mite under the weather lately. That is to say she had been astayin' in bed 'til almost daybreak rather than gettin' up at her regular hour of 4 a.m. So Little Red was acarryin' her some fresh baked bread and some homemade pear preserves.

I'm No Sleeping Beauty...

Now Little Red was strollin' through a cactus patch when she spied a varmit, Dirty Dan McWolfe, who jest happened to be the most wanted varmit in the territory. 'Course Little Red didn't know that. She jest knew she hadn't seen this stranger 'round town before and he didn't look none too trustworthy. But bein' polite, and a good-sized girl who could take care of herself, Little Red said, "Howdy."

Dirty Dan was a scoundrel but not stupid. After all he had managed to pull off a long string of robberies without gettin' caught. Not wantin' to alarm Little Red and draw unnecessary attention to his whereabouts, Dirty Dan minded his manners. He tipped his hat and said, "Howdy, Little Lady. Where might you be headed?"

"I'm going to sit a spell with my Granny at the Lazy A. She's been feeling poorly lately."

"Thunderation, Little Lady, you oughta pick a bunch of them purty wildflowers over yonder. I bet yore Granny would be tickled pink to have 'em. I know my Granny shore would."

Little Red thanked the stranger and walked over to the patch of wildflowers. She wondered why she had not thought of that herself, because her Granny did love flowers.

While Little Red was apickin' the flowers, Dirty Dan hightailed it to the Lazy A. The train he planned to rob wadn't due 'til tomorrow and ever'body knew the Lazy A was one of the richest spreads in the territory. With nobody 'round 'cept an old lady, one that had been sickly at that, it would be easy pickin'.

Granny was on the lookout for Little Red. Lookin' out the winder rather than seein' Little Red like she 'spected she spied Dirty Dan McWolfe. Granny recognized him right off 'cause she read the wanted posters ever' time she went to the post office. There was a whole pile of Dirty Dan posters by now. Well, jest 'cause Granny was on up in years didn't mean she was stupid. Jest 'cause she could handle a gun as good as any man didn't mean she took unnecessary risks. So when Granny saw Dirty Dan aheadin' her way, she did the smart thing and hid in the root cellar.

Dirty Dan kicked open the door only to find the house plum empty. He had heard the stories 'bout the money the old lady was s'posed to have stashed away. He didn't worry much 'bout where the old lady was; he was after her money. He was so busy diggin' through drawers lookin' for gold he didn't hear Little Red come in 'til it was way too late.

Dirty Dan never knew what hit him. When he came to, he was alayin' on the floor, bound hand and foot, with Granny astandin' over him holdin' her trusty six shooter. Now Dirty Dan never knew what hit him, but I'm agoin' to tell you. Little Red hit him upside the head with that loaf of fresh baked bread she had in her basket. Nobody ever claimed

Little Red could cook worth a hoot. That there bread couldn't be et, but it shore come in handy as a weapon. Once Dirty Dan was bound up hand and foot, Little Red and Granny tossed him in the back of the wagon and headed toward town.

Pullin' up in front of the sheriff's office, Little Red and Granny were greeted by Deputy Dixon. Deputy Dixon was a mite surprised to see the most wanted varmit in the territory had been captured by two women armed only with a loaf of bread. 'Course knowin' Granny and Little Red twarn't yore regular run of the mill women, it didn't surprise him all that much.

Last I heard tell Granny was back at the Lazy A, feelin' purty pert and thinkin' serious like 'bout runnin' fer sheriff. Dirty Dan had a nice little cell all to hisself in the brand new jail. From his winder he had a real good view of the train depot. Seems like Little Red and Deputy Dixon hit it off right nice, and they started showin' up together at barn dances and ice cream socials and whatnot.

It jest goes to show you can't know somebody by lookin' at 'em. You don't go pokin' yore nose in somebody's drawers lessen you're invited in. And you shore don't want to cross a lady carryin' a loaf of fresh baked bread.

Chicky Nicky

You see a friend running down the street yelling the sky is falling. He offers no proof. You ask for none. You immediately fall in behind him and begin predicting the end of the world. If you are not careful you just might be right. When you become part of the crowd you risk getting stepped on—or worse.

Chicky Nicky loved his big-screen television. He had a satellite dish that brought in more than two hundred channels. Chicky Nicky was no dummy; he did not watch only sporting events. He watched the news every night. He never missed "Aliens Among Us"; he had every episode on tape.

One day as Chicky Nicky was walking to the mailbox, something hit him on the head. Hard. Chicky Nicky was well informed. He knew what it was. The sky was falling. He didn't know if something had fallen through the hole in the ozone layer or if something had fallen from a passing alien craft. All he knew was the sky was falling. He had to tell someone.

Chicky Nicky ran down the street. He met Henny Denny.

Henny Denny said, "Where's the fire?"

Chicky Nicky said, "Henny Denny, the sky is falling. A piece of it just hit me on the head. We have to tell someone."

Henny Denny said, "We must hurry. We must tell someone."

Henny Denny and Chicky Nicky ran down the street. They met Ducky Bucky.

Ducky Bucky said, "What's the rush?"

Henny Denny said, "Ducky Bucky, the sky is falling."

Chicky Nicky said, "Yes, the sky is falling. A piece of it just hit me on the head. We have to tell someone."

Ducky Bucky said, "We must hurry. We must tell someone." Ducky Bucky, Henny Denny and Chicky Nicky ran down the street. They met Goosey Moosey.

Goosey Moosey said, "What's the hurry?"

Ducky Bucky said, "Goosey Moosey, the sky is falling."

Henny Denny said, "The sky is falling.

Chicky Nicky said, "Yes, the sky is falling. A piece of it just hit me on the head. We have to tell someone."

Goosey Moosey said, "We must hurry. We must tell someone."

Goosey Moosey, Ducky Bucky, Henny Denny and Chicky Nicky ran down the street. They met Turkey Hurkey.

Turkey Hurkey said, "What's happening?"

Goosey Moosey said, "Turkey

Hurkey, the sky is falling."

Ducky Bucky said, "The sky is falling."

Henny Denny said, "The sky is falling."

Chicky Nicky said, "Yes, the sky is falling. A piece of it just hit me on the head. We have to tell someone."

Turkey Hurkey said, "We must hurry. We must tell someone."

Turkey Hurkey, Goosey Moosey, Ducky Bucky, Henny Denny and Chicky Nicky ran down the street. They met Foxy Moxy.

Foxy Moxy said, "What's the problem?"

Turkey Hurkey said, "Foxy Moxy, the sky is falling."

Goosey Moosey said, "The sky is falling."

Ducky Bucky said, "The sky is falling."

Henny Denny said, "The sky is falling."

Chicky Nicky said, "Yes, the sky is

falling. A piece of it just hit me on the head. We have to tell someone."

Foxy Moxy said, "Please, tell me all about it."

Turkey Hurkey, Goosey Moosey, Ducky Bucky, Henny Denny and Chicky Nicky followed Foxy Moxy into her house. If the sky did fall, they never knew it.

Rule number one: Don't believe everything you see on your big-screen television.

Rule number two: Don't repeat rumors.

Rule number three: Don't follow the crowd.

Rule number four: Don't trust every strange fox you meet. You might end up in a stew pot.

The Great Rutabaga

You want to have some fun? Get a group of kids and act out this story. They love pulling and tugging on the pretend rutabaga. Be prepared for moans and groans when you talk about how good rutabagas are, especially rutabaga ice cream. Kids will let you know in a minute they think that is disgusting. Kids are so great because they are so honest and say exactly what they mean. Too bad we can't stay kids.

Archie loved rutabagas better than anything. He liked sweet rutabagas, sour rutabagas, candied rutabagas, pickled rutabagas, rutabaga dumplings, rutabaga bread, rutabaga pie, rutabaga cake and rutabaga cookies, but his absolute favorite, favorite food was rutabaga ice cream. Bless your heart, do you mean to tell me you don't like rutabaga ice cream? You just do not know what is good!

Since Archie loved rutabagas so much he decided to plant an entire field of rutabagas. He was going to have all the rutabagas he wanted. He planted those rutabagas and waited. Before long that field was full of rutabaga plants. Most rutabagas grow to be about so high. Well, this one rutabaga grew and grew and grew. Pretty soon it was as tall as Archie! Law a mercy, Archie had never seen a rutabaga that big. He decided he better get it out of the ground before it got too big to be gotten. Archie put on his work boots and went out in field. He grabbed hold of that rutabaga and he took a deep breath and he pulled. Nothing happened. That rutabaga did not budge. Archie looked around and he saw his wife, Betty Nell, hanging clothes on the line so he called her over to help.

Archie grabbed hold of that ruta-baga. Betty Nell grabbed hold of Archie. They took a deep breath and they pulled. Nothing. That rutabaga did not budge. Archie looked around and he saw his boy, Charlie Joe, down by the barn so he called Charlie Joe over to help.

Archie grabbed hold of that ruta-baga. Betty Nell grabbed hold of Archie. Charlie Joe grabbed hold of Betty Nell. They took a deep breath and they pulled. Nothing happened. That rutabaga did not budge. Archie looked around and he saw his girl, Dottie May, down by the creek so he called Dottie May over to help.

Archie grabbed hold of that ruta-baga. Betty Nell grabbed hold of Archie. Charlie Joe grabbed hold of Betty Nell. Dottie May grabbed hold of Charlie Joe. They took a deep breath and they pulled. Nothing happened. That rutabaga did not budge. Archie had his whole family helping him and he still couldn't pull up that rutabaga. What was he going to do? He looked around and he saw his old hound dog, Elvis, lying under the porch so he called Elvis over to help.

Archie grabbed hold of that rutabaga. Betty Nell grabbed hold of Archie. Charlie Joe grabbed hold of Betty Nell. Dottie May grabbed hold of Charlie Joe. Elvis the hound dog grabbed hold of Dottie May. They took a deep breath and they pulled. Nothing happened. That rutabaga did not budge. Archie looked around and he saw the cat, Freida, asleep in the sun so he called Freida over to help.

Archie grabbed hold of that rutabaga. Betty Nell grabbed hold of Archie. Charlie Joe grabbed hold of Betty Nell. Dottie May grabbed hold of Charlie Joe. Elvis the hound dog grabbed hold of Dottie May. Freida the cat grabbed hold of Elvis the hound dog. They took a deep breath and they pulled. Nothing happened. That rutabaga did not budge.

Archie was stumped. He had his

whole family and all his animals help-ing him and he still couldn't pull up that rutabaga. What was he going to do? He was standing there, scratching his head, when along came a little bitty ole possum just poking along.

Pauline Possum saw all those great big people and animals standing around. She stopped and asked what they were doing. Archie told her they were trying to pull up that big ole rutabaga. Pauline Possum thought that sounded like fun and begged Archie to let her join in . Archie said she was too small to be of any help, but Pauline Possum kept begging until Archie gave in. Archie told Pauline Possum to go to the end of the line and grab hold of Freida the cat's tail.

Archie grabbed hold of the ruta-baga. Betty Nell grabbed hold of Archie. Charlie Joe grabbed hold of Betty Nell. Dottie May grabbed hold of Charlie Joe. Elvis the hound dog grabbed hold of Dottie May. Freida the cat grabbed hold of Elvis the hound dog. Pauline Possum grabbed hold of Freida the cat. They took a deep breath and they pulled. At first nothing happened. Then there was a low rumbling noise that got louder and louder. All of a sudden that rutabaga popped clean out of the ground.

That rutabaga was so big they couldn't pick it up. They had to roll it to the house. When they got it to the house it wouldn't fit through the door. They had to wash it off with the hose and cut it up before they could get it into the house. They filled every pot in the house with rutabaga. They cooked rutabaga and they cooked rutabaga.

That night Archie and his family sat down to a rutabaga feast. Pauline Possum was guest of honor because it was thanks to her that the rutabaga finally came out of the ground. They had sweet rutabagas, sour rutabagas, candied rutabagas, pickled rutabagas, rutabaga dumplings, rutabaga bread, rutabaga pie, rutabaga cake and rutabaga cookies. For dessert they had rutabaga ice cream. They ate rutabaga ice cream and they ate rutabaga ice cream. Do you know how many bowls of rutabaga ice cream Pauline Possum ate? Let me tell you. Thirty-four. Yes, Pauline Possum ate thirty-four bowls of rutabaga ice cream!

I want you to remember the next time you go to the store for rutabaga ice cream how hard Archie and his family worked to make rutabaga ice cream just for you.

Always remember it is what is inside, not your size, that counts.

Duff the Dancing Dragon

This is a book of fairy tales. There has to be a dragon story. Of course, it is not going to be a normal dragon story. There will be no fighting, no violence. Traditionally dragons are thought of as large, fierce, clumsy and terrifying. I prefer to think of my dragon as a dancer. A two-stepping dragon with a sense of humor.

Ting Kurt was bored. He employed many capable people who did their jobs so well there was little for him to do. Being king was largely ceremonial: public appearances, ribbon cuttings, awarding prizes at the annual fair. But most of these events occurred in the fall, and now it was summer. The villagers were hard at work in the fields and forest. Castle employees were taking their annual vacations. No one had time for ceremonies. No one had time for the king. King Kurt was bored.

The king decided to visit his daughter, Panda. Being with her made him happy. She would know how to entertain him and chase away his boredom.

Princess Panda rushed to greet King Kurt as he entered her chambers. "Oh, Papa, I am so glad you are here. I am so bored! I cannot think of one thing to do. You are the king. Make my boredom go away!"

"Panda, I was hoping you could help me. I am bored too,.

"When you were my age what did people do when they were bored?"

"People didn't have time to be bored. There were many dragons then, roaming freely about the country and terrorizing everyone. A knight would ride from the castle and challenge the dragon. A fierce battle would follow, sometimes lasting all day. Finally the dragon would be defeated. Most were killed, but some were driven into caves in the mountains. Then there would be a great victory celebration that would last for days. Eventually another dragon would come along and there would be another battle followed by another victory celebration. An on and on and on. Now all the dragons have been defeated and no longer roam the countryside. All the knights have retired to Miami."

"Papa, I've never seen a knight battle a dragon. Actually, I've never seen a knight or a dragon. If only there were wild dragons today! I have an idea. I just saw an ad in the newspaper: "Doug's Rent-a-Dragon. Dragons for all occasions. No event too large or too small." We can hire a dragon to attack the castle. A brave young man from the village will rush to battle the dragon and defend the castle. When he has defeated the dragon, you can knight him and we will have a huge celebration, with dancing. Papa, it will be just like the old days. It will be so much fun. I'm going to call Doug's Rent-a-Dragon right now."

Panda dashed out the door, leaving the king alone. He walked toward the garden as he tried to recall the knighting ceremony. It had been a long time since he had been required to knight anyone. While the king sat, pondering, a young man rushed into the garden. He was very excited, having seen a dragon heading toward the castle. Being a sensible young man, he had rushed to the castle to alert the king.

King Kurt was thrilled. He had no idea a dragon would be found this quickly. Panda had been right; this would be fun. He began instructing the young man on the finer points of dragon fighting.

The young man had other ideas.

"Fight a dragon! Are you crazy? I'm a miller, not a knight. You're the king. It's your job to defend us. I'm going home to hide in the cellar until the dragon is gone." He exited, quickly.

Hide in the cellar! The king was shocked. That was not a very brave thing to do. Of course, if a huge, fierce dragon were headed toward the castle that might not be a bad idea. Dragons should not be taken lightly and, after all, he was a king, not a knight. He was a ruler, not a fighter. Perhaps he should check the castle's cellar, just to make sure it had a full stock of emergency supplies. The king exited, quickly.

Duff the Dragon sauntered into the empty garden. Since retiring from active dragoning he had been employed by Doug's Rent-a-Dragon to entertain at parties. Humans loved to hear stories from his fighting days. He assumed there was to be a royal party that required entertainment. Finding no one, Duff sat down and waited.

Princess Panda rushed into the garden, clipboard in hand. She was at her best organizing people and events, and she had a long list of things to be done. She was thrilled to see Duff. Now the fun could begin.

Duff stood and bowed a low bow, very politely and totally unexpected from a dragon. "I am Duff the Dragon and I am here to entertain your guests."

Panda stared at Duff. He was not what she had expected. "It's not a party, exactly. You don't look like I thought you would. You're not a very fierce-looking dragon. My goodness, you're not even breathing fire!"

"Breathing fire? Of course not. It's bad for my health. I gave it up long ago."

"Well, I suppose you will do. You are to pretend to attack the castle. When everyone sees we are under siege, a brave young man will rush to defend us. There will be a huge battle, which, of course, you will lose. Please, try to look menacing. I will pay extra if you will breathe fire. After you are defeated we will have a huge celebration, with dancing. We will all live happily ever after."

"Wait a minute, hold the phone. You want me to do what? This is not the type of party I was expecting. *I* won't live happily ever after if I am defeated. You do not understand. I do not fight anymore. I could get hurt.

"I promise you will not be seriously hurt. What kind of dragon are you? Dragons are supposed to fight knights."

"Says who? What kind of dragon am I? I'm a smart dragon. I don't like fighting. People get hurt. I could get hurt. I am retired. End of discussion."

"Retired? Isn't that boring? What do you do when you get bored?"

"I don't get bored. I have lots of things to do. If I should begin to feel bored, I dance. That always ends my boredom."

"I love to dance, but today it is so expensive to arrange a ball."

"For a princess, you're not very

smart. You do not need a formal ball in order to dance. Just get up and dance." Duff leapt to his feet and began to dance. He swayed; he hopped; he bopped; he dipped; he spun. He moved exceptionally well for a dragon.

Panda was thrilled. She had not thought of dragons as dancers. Here was a dragon, in her garden, dancing. Not only was he dancing, he was doing steps Panda had never seen. She asked him to please teach her the new steps. Panda and Duff were having so much fun they did not see King Kurt enter the garden. He was stopped dead in his tracks by the sight of his daughter dancing with a dragon.

Duff and Panda paused to catch their breath.

"Duff, you must come live in the castle," Panda said. "You can be my dance teacher and show me all the latest steps. It will be so much fun I will never be bored again."

King Kurt rushed to his daughter.

"Panda, what are you thinking? You can't have a dragon living in the castle. What will people think? Dragons attack castles; they do not live in them."

Duff drew himself to his full height. "I do not think I want to live in a castle, or be a dance teacher. I am a dragon. I may no longer attack castles, but I still have my pride."

"Papa, Duff, both of you stop being silly. We are not living in the dark ages. People change; dragons change. Papa, it would be fun to have a dancing dragon in the castle. Duff, you would have a nice soft bed. No more sleeping in caves. Regular meals. No one would ask you to fight knights."

"No fighting. Soft bed. Regular meals. Life in a castle might not be so bad. I could learn to like it. I suppose I could learn to like being a dancing dragon."

"Papa, if Duff lives here we can show everyone humans and dragons can live together and be friends. I bet there are a lot of projects they could work on together. Of course, as king, you would be in charge. You would never be bored again."

The king thought that was a splendid idea. So happy he had thought of such a brilliant idea, he rushed off to write down his thoughts and plans.

Duff moved into the castle. He loved his apartment, especially the soft, warm bed. He was overjoyed when he learned the royal cook could make blueberry pies. He loved, dearly loved, blueberry pies. Duff found living in a castle was a pretty good deal.

Once everyone stopped looking at each other as enemies and instead saw each other as individuals they realized they had much in common. Everyone wants to be useful, loved, appreciated and accepted as they are. Having an endless supply of your dessert is just the icing on the cake.

The Industrious Hen

The moral of this story says it all: If you think you can't, you can't. If you think you can, you can. Believe in yourself. Don't let anyone tell you what you are capable of. You may not be a Sleeping Beauty or a Prince Charming—few of us are. But everyone is unique and special. Be your own fairy godperson. Believe in yourself and make your dreams come true— today.

The hen found several grains of corn in the barnyard. Being a smart hen she knew if she ate the grain she would have only one meal. However, if she planted the grain and grew her own corn she would have many meals. The hen thought this was an excellent idea.

She asked her friend the turkey to help her.

Her good friend the turkey listened, but she really did not understand. Why should they do all that work when the farmer fed them everyday? They did not have to feed themselves. The turkey did not understand what the hen meant by the satisfaction of self-reliance. The turkey said no.

The hen asked her good friend the goose to help plant the grain. The goose said she did not know anything about gardening. The hen said she could learn. The goose really was not interested in learning anything new. Also she didn't think gardening was something a goose needed to know. The goose said no.

The hen asked her good friend the duck to help plant the grain. The duck really did not have time. She had bugs to catch and little ducks to feed, and the ducklings had swimming lessons. She just did not have time. The hen said if she did this she could spend less time searching for food and more time with her ducklings. The duck just did not have time to think about it right now. She said no.

The hen asked her good friend the rooster to help plant the grain. The rooster chuckled and patted her on the head. He said that while the idea sounded good it really needed some work. Obviously the hen did not know anything about agriculture. If she would just leave the grain with him he would think about it and let her know how the idea could be improved. The hen said no. She would do it herself, alone, her way.

She did. While everyone else was running around scratching in the barnyard, in search of food, the hen was able to relax and enjoy the fruits of her labor.

While her friends thought they couldn't, or shouldn't, the industrious hen knew she could and did. Whether you think you can or you can't, you're right!

Cate Howard
Storyteller

Cate Howard began her career in community theatre, progressed to puppeteer and finally got her act together as a storyteller.

Entertaining ages three and up in settings ranging from birthday parties to Birmingham, Alabama's City Stages, Cate also conducts workshops for children and adults. Whether your organization numbers ten or one thousand and whatever the age range, Cate has a program for you. Believing laughter is the key to successful living, Cate will entertain and inspire you.

To discuss scheduling Cate Howard for your upcoming event, call 615-591-4018.